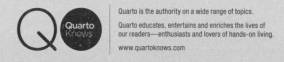

Quarto is the authority on a wide range of topics.

Quarto educates, entertains and enriches the lives of
our readers—enthusiasts and lovers of hands-on living.

www.quartoknows.com

First Published in 2020 by words & pictures,

an imprint of The Quarto Group.

26391 Crown Valley Parkway, Suite 220, Mission Viejo, CA 92691, USA

T: +1 949 380 7510

F: +1 949 380 7575

www.quartoknows.com

A CIP record for this book is available from the Library of Congress.

Original edition in French by Actes Sud Junior

© Actes Sud Junior 2018

ISBN: 978 0 7112 5529 6

9 8 7 6 5 4 3

Manufactured in Guangdong, China TT052021

I ALWAYS WANTED ONE

Olivier Tallec

words & pictures

I always wanted one.

So, that morning, when I saw him there,

I could not believe my eyes!

I got a little bit closer

and my heart beat a little bit faster.

I could see right away how cute he was,

with his big beautiful eyes! But he was so shy

at first. We had to get to know each other.

It's often like that with new friends.

In the beginning, I wanted him to sleep in my house.

We tried but it was impossible!

He refused to sleep and he took up ALL the room!

We decided he should sleep in the cat's house.

It's very big and is right next to mine.

That way, he's not far away.

I tried to teach him how to eat on the floor,

like everybody else, but he prefers the table.

He's a really fussy eater...he doesn't like anything!

I just think it's weird that he doesn't like dry food.

He was terrible at washing himself, too!

But once he's dried off, he's all soft and warm...

And lucky for him, I love brushing his hair.

So it wasn't always easy,

but then we found this game we love.

He throws a stick and I get it and give

it back. Then he throws it again. And again...

We can play for hours! Well, HE loves it, but I have

to say, it gets quite boring after a while.

He doesn't behave himself all the time...

he keeps on running away!

I can spend the whole day looking for him.

He always comes back eventually.

Still, I wonder, where does he go all day?

It's the same when we go on vacation,

I'm always scared I'll lose him.

But it's never for long.

At home, the couch is MY spot.

I don't really like it when he climbs up to join me.

But sometimes, when we're watching the TV

together and eating chips, he falls asleep.

And that's quite cute.

And I must walk him every day, even when it's raining!

If he stays in all day, he tends to get frustrated.

But I like to show him off. All my friends have

one too, but I think mine is the best one.

I know he was a gift, which is great, but I sometimes wish I could have picked him myself. There are just so many of them to choose from! It's fine though, he's still cool. And anyway, I think we quite like each other.

We've known each other for a long time now—years, even!

He's grown bigger and takes up ALL the room on MY couch.

He still doesn't like dry food, and he still loves that stick game...

But we remain the best of friends in the world.